TM

Note to parents, carers and teachers

Read it yourself is a series of modern stories, favourite characters and traditional tales written in a simple way for children who are learning to read. The books can be read independently or as part of a guided reading session.

Each book is carefully structured to include many high-frequency words vital for first reading. The sentences on each page are supported closely by pictures to help with understanding, and to offer lively details to talk about.

The books are graded into four levels that progressively introduce wider vocabulary and longer stories as a reader's ability and confidence grows.

Ideas for use

- Begin by looking through the book and talking about the pictures. Has your child heard this story before?

- Help your child with any words he does not know, either by helping him to sound them out or supplying them yourself.

- Developing readers can be concentrating so hard on the words that they sometimes don't fully grasp the meaning of what they're reading. Answering the puzzle questions on pages 30 and 31 will help with understanding.

For more information and advice on Read it yourself and book banding, visit www.ladybird.com/readityourself

Book Band 7

Level 2 is ideal for children who have received some reading instruction and can read short, simple sentences with help.

Special features:

Frequent repetition of main story words and phrases

Short, simple sentences

Jemima Puddle-duck lived on a farm.

She wanted to make a nest and hatch her eggs, but the farmer's wife took her eggs away.

6

7

Large, clear type

Careful match between story and pictures

"I am looking for a good, safe place to hatch my eggs," said Jemima. "The farm is not safe."

"I can help you," said the gentleman. "My shed is a safe place to make a nest. You can hide in there."

16

17

Educational Consultant: Geraldine Taylor
Book Banding Consultant: Kate Ruttle

LADYBIRD BOOKS

UK | USA | Canada | Ireland | Australia
India | New Zealand | South Africa

Ladybird Books is part of the Penguin Random House group of companies
whose addresses can be found at global.penguinrandomhouse.com.

www.penguin.co.uk   www.puffin.co.uk   www.ladybird.co.uk

Penguin
Random House
UK

Read it yourself with Ladybird: The Tale of Jemima Puddle-Duck first published 2013
This edition published 2017
001

Read it yourself with Ladybird: The Tale of Jemima Puddle-Duck text based on the original tale by
Beatrix Potter © Frederick Warne & Co., 2013
New reproductions of Beatrix Potter's book illustrations copyright © Frederick Warne & Co., 2002
Original text and illustrations copyright © Frederick Warne & Co., 1908
Peter RabbitTM & Beatrix PotterTM Frederick Warne & Co.
Frederick Warne & Co. is the owner of all rights, copyrights and trademarks
in the Beatrix Potter character names and illustrations.

Printed in China

A CIP catalogue record for this book is available from the British Library

ISBN: 978–0–723–27343–1

All correspondence to:
Ladybird Books
Penguin Random House Children's
80 Strand, London WC2R 0RL

The Tale of Jemima Puddle-Duck

based on the original tale
by Beatrix Potter

Jemima Puddle-duck
lived on a farm.

She wanted to make
a nest and hatch her eggs,
but the farmer's wife took
her eggs away.

Jemima Puddle-duck
tried to hide her eggs
on the farm, but the
farmer's wife took her
eggs away again.

One day, Jemima left
the farm to lay some
eggs where she knew
the farmer's wife
could not find them.

Jemima Puddle-duck
went to a wood.

The wood looked like a
good place to make her
nest and lay some eggs.

In the wood, Jemima
looked for a safe place
to lay her eggs.

But there was a gentleman
in the wood.

"Where are you going?"
said the gentleman.

"I am looking for a good, safe place to hatch my eggs," said Jemima. "The farm is not safe."

"I can help you," said the gentleman. "My shed is a safe place to make a nest. You can hide in there."

Jemima liked the shed.
She made a nest and
laid her eggs.

One day, the gentleman said to Jemima, "Would you like to have dinner with me? Go back to the farm to get some herbs and then we can have dinner."

Jemima saw a dog
on the farm.
"I am going to have
dinner with a gentleman,"
she said.

But the dog knew that the
gentleman was a fox.
He went to get some other
dogs to help.

Jemima went back
to the shed.

The gentleman said,
"Come to my house when
you have seen to the eggs,
and we will have dinner."

When Jemima was safe in
the shed with her eggs,
the dogs ran to the
gentleman fox's house.

The fox saw the dogs
coming and ran away.
He did not come back.

The dogs took Jemima
Puddle-duck back to the
farm. She made a safe nest
and laid her eggs. These
eggs did hatch!

How much do you remember about
The Tale of Jemima Puddle-Duck?
Answer these questions and find out!

- ## Why does Jemima leave the farm?

- ## Who does Jemima meet in the wood?

- ## Where does the gentleman fox say Jemima can lay her eggs?

- ## Who takes Jemima back to the farm?

TM

Look at the pictures and match them to the character names.

Jemima Puddle-duck

gentleman fox

farmer's wife

dog

Tick the books you've read!

Level 1

☐ ☐ ☐ ☐ ☐

☐ ☐ ☐ ☐ ☐

Level 2

☐ ☐ ☐ ☐ ☐

☐ ☐ ☐ ☐ ☐

Level 3

☐ ☐ ☐ ☐ ☐

Level 4

☐ ☐ ☐ ☐ ☐